# Dear Parents:

Congratulations! Your child is taking
the first steps on an exciting journey.
The destination? Independent reading!

STEP INTO READING® will help your child get there. The program offers
five steps to reading success. Each step includes fun stories and colorful
art or photographs. In addition to original fiction and books with favorite
characters, there are Step into Reading Non-Fiction Readers, Phonics Readers
and Boxed Sets, Sticker Readers, and Comic Readers—a complete literacy
program with something to interest every child.

## Learning to Read, Step by Step!

### Ready to Read   Preschool–Kindergarten
• big type and easy words • rhyme and rhythm • picture clues
For children who know the alphabet and are eager to
begin reading.

### Reading with Help   Preschool–Grade 1
• basic vocabulary • short sentences • simple stories
For children who recognize familiar words and sound out
new words with help.

### Reading on Your Own   Grades 1–3
• engaging characters • easy-to-follow plots • popular topics
For children who are ready to read on their own.

### Reading Paragraphs   Grades 2–3
• challenging vocabulary • short paragraphs • exciting stories
For newly independent readers who read simple sentences
with confidence.

### Ready for Chapters   Grades 2–4
• chapters • longer paragraphs • full-color art
For children who want to take the plunge into chapter books
but still like colorful pictures.

STEP INTO READING® is designed to give every child a successful
reading experience. The grade levels are only guides; children will progress
through the steps at their own speed, developing confidence in their reading.

Remember, a lifetime love of reading starts with a single step!

Visit us on the Web!
StepIntoReading.com
randomhousekids.com

Educators and librarians, for a variety of teaching tools, visit us at RHTeachersLibrarians.com

ISBN 978-1-5247-2068-1 (trade) — ISBN 978-1-5247-2069-8 (lib. bdg.)

Printed in the United States of America

10 9 8 7 6 5 4 3 2 1

nickelodeon

RUSTY RIVETS

# Magnet Power!

by Tex Huntley

based on the teleplay
"Rusty Digs In" by Ravi Steve

illustrated by Donald Cassity

Random House 🏠 New York

Today is an
important day
for Rusty.

His friend Mr. Higgins
will get a medal!
Mr. Higgins is the
town's first inventor.

Rusty made the medal.
It is gold and shiny.

Oh, no!

The medal is missing.

Rusty thinks

Botasaur buried it.

How can Rusty and Ruby
check all the holes
in the yard?

Maybe Rusty's
really powerful magnet
can find the medal.

The magnet finds cans,
plane wings, and even Jack.
It does not find the medal.
Botasaur did not bury it.

Rusty puts
a metal detector
on Ruby's buggy.

Now they can search
all over town.
Time to bolt!

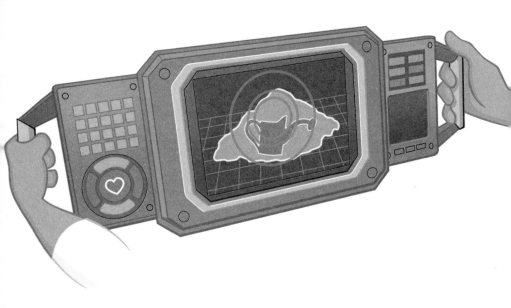

*Beep. Beep. Beep.*

The metal detector
does not find the medal.

A seagull flies overhead.

*Beep. Beep. BEEP!*

The seagull has the medal!

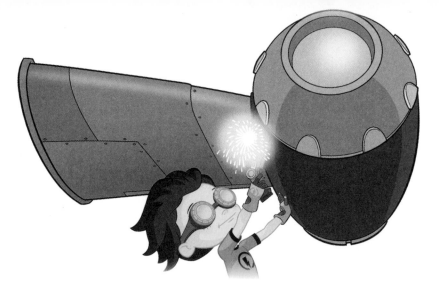

Let's combine it
and design it!
Rusty puts the magnet and
plane wings on Botasaur.

Rusty and Botasaur

take off!

Rusty and Botasaur
go after the seagull.
They fly higher
and higher.

Botasaur gets the medal
with the magnet.

Botasaur and Rusty
reach the stage
just in time!

Ranger Anna gives
Mr. Higgins the medal.

Hooray for Mr. Higgins!

Botasaur is a hero!
Rusty makes a really big
medal for him.

# Botasaur buries his medal!

# Hooray for Botasaur!